With *thanks to Ron and Atie*

THIS IS A BORZOI BOOK PUBLISHED BY ALFRED A. KNOPF, INC.
Copyright © 1997 by Babette Cole
Published in the United States by Alfred A. Knopf, Inc., New York, and simultaneously in Canada
by Random House of Canada Limited, Toronto. Distributed by Random House, Inc., New York.
Originally published as *Two of Everything* in Great Britain in 1997 by Jonathan Cape Limited,
Random House UK Limited.

http://www.randomhouse.com/

First American edition, 1998

Library of Congress Cataloging-in-Publication Data
Cole, Babette.
The un-wedding / by Babette Cole
p.   cm.
Summary: As their parents disagree more and more about everything,
Demetrius and Paula Ogglebutt decide that everyone would be happier if they "un-marry."
ISBN 0-679-88898-5
|1. Divorce—Fiction. 2. Parent and child—Fiction.| I. Title.
PZ7.C6734Tx
1998 |E|—dc21
97-13854
Printed in Singapore
10 9 8 7 6 5 4 3 2 1

The Un-Wedding

Babette Cole

Alfred A. Knopf New York

Demetrius and Paula Ogglebutt were
two perfectly beautiful children...

but...

they had two problem parents who could never agree about anything.

Their opinions were never the same about anything.

Dad's idea of a holiday.

Dad's idea of a dog. →

Dad's idea of art.

Mum's idea of a holiday. →

Mum's idea of a dog. →

Mum's idea of art.

The longer Mr. and Mrs. Ogglebutt lived together,
the more they disliked each other.

They had started off as quite good-looking parents.

But because they had ugly thoughts about each other...
it began to show and they became uglier and uglier.

They started playing tricks on each other: Mr. Ogglebutt put concrete powder in his wife's bath salts!

She put fireworks in his sausages and mashed potatoes!

To get even, he buried
wrigglers in her mudpack!

Then she hid a present from one
of his cows in his cap!

And he boiled her underwear
until it shrank!

Paula and Demetrius became worried by their parents' behavior. They thought it might be their fault.

They were very sad and confused.

They decided to see if anyone else at their school had the same problem.

Loads of kids turned up! They all agreed that it was not their fault if their parents behaved like five-year-olds.

"What do we do about it?" said Demetrius.
"I've got an idea," said Paula.

So they went to see the minister to ask if
he could un-marry their parents.

"What a clever idea," said the minister. "You know, it might be the only thing they will *ever* agree about!"

"Brilliant!" said their parents.
"Why didn't *we* think of that?"

"Because you are always
arguing," said Paula and
Demetrius.

They had lots of
things to organize...

like sending out the
un-wedding invitations

and ordering the
un-wedding cake.

The un-wedding was a joyous occasion for everyone.

Once their parents had jetted off on their separate un-honeymoons...

Demetrius and Paula bulldozed the house as an un-wedding present.

In its place they built two separate houses—one to suit each parent.

These were connected by a secret tunnel—big enough only for
Demetrius and Paula.

And, of course, because they now lived in two houses,
they ordered two of everything they wanted.

They also ended up with two very contented parents who could live happily ever after—apart.

The End